The Singapore Slayings

Bob Haider

Published by Bob Haider, 2024.

This is a work of fiction. Similarities to real people, places, or events are entirely coincidental.

THE SINGAPORE SLAYINGS

First edition. July 18, 2024.

Copyright © 2024 Bob Haider.

ISBN: 979-8227850676

Written by Bob Haider.

Dedicated to my friend, Jeffrey Ho

Prologue

Captain Baskin arose from his chair and walked to the glass door of his office.

Whenever the soft-spoken captain arose, invariably those detectives who weren't on the phone noticed the intimidating six-foot, three-inch figure standing in the doorway.

Lieutenant Barton was one of several detectives who noticed the massive figure in the doorframe and Barton saw the captain's curling index finger beckoning him, so he immediately headed toward the captain's office.

As Barton entered, Captain Baskin closed the door behind him, and said, "Have a seat."

He did so in one of two chairs as his captain moved around his desk and sat down his chair.

"What's up, Captain?"

Baskin shook his head.

Oh boy, here it comes, thought Barton.

"Sometimes I wish you weren't so damn good!"

"How's that, sir?"

"God knows we have plenty of cases for you to work on here," he said, as he glanced at a three-inch thick manila folder lying on his desk.

Barton looked at the captain questioningly, and commented, "I take it I'm heading somewhere."

"Yeah, you're on loan again. It's all in the file here."

Barton smiled that confident smile of his that soon evolved into a smirk. Being loaned out had occurred several times over the past few years. Barton, the fifty-two-year-old lieutenant in the Chicago police department, had developed quite a reputation as a homicide detective over the years. Whenever one of the woefully inexperienced and under staffed police departments in the Chicago suburbs needed some assistance, someone invariably made a call.

"Where are we heading this time, captain...north...south...west?" asked Barton, as he omitted the one direction that would put him in the middle of Lake Michigan.

"Not we, just you. Your partner, Sergeant Crawford will be staying here."

"Oh, okay. So, where to?"

"Uh," the captain stammered, "west. "You'll be heading west," he replied with a furrowed brow.

"Damn!" Barton replied. He lived within the city limits of Chicago and was hoping it was not too far out in the burbs. "Another long commute, hey? How far out this time? Des Plaines? Elgin?"

"Uh...a bit farther than that, I'm afraid," Captain Baskin remarked.

"You're not sending me to Rockford again! That's so damn far out!"

Baskin smiled sympathetically, but not wishing to prolong Barton's queries any longer, he answered bluntly, "It appears your reputation goes far beyond the Chicago Metropolitan area. Get your passport out, lieutenant. You're heading to the Land of Orchids."

"Huh?"

"You're going to Singapore."

"What?"

"Yeah, Singapore officials contacted the U.S. Embassy for assistance...very quietly, very unofficially," said Baskin, as he patted the thick manila folder.

"The contents of this crime book were sent from Singapore via the overnight diplomatic pouch. It has the highest priority. They said under no circumstances will anyone be allowed access to their database while you're over the Pacific, which means we can't assist you from here. Whether they allow you into their database once you get there, who knows."

The captain slid the manila folder toward Barton. "There's been a series of murders. You'll need to familiarize yourself with the case while you're enroute and that's all you'll have until you arrive in Singapore."

"Is it complete?" Barton asked, as he eyed the folder.

Baskin shrugged, "They say yes, but who knows?"

"I don't get it, captain. Why not the FBI, or the CIA...or even Army Intelligence? Wouldn't a federal agency be a more likely choice in assisting a foreign government?"

"The Prime Minister of Singapore said absolutely no government involvement. He wants to keep this as quiet as possible, but, beyond that, he wants a bona fide homicide detective to figure out what's happening over there and catch the bastard."

"Oh?"

"Yeah, the Prime Minister personally asked for you."

Barton emitted an exasperated sigh.

"Yeah," Baskin agreed. "It sucks bein' good at your job, doesn't it? Anyway, he said he wanted you, and no one else but you."

"No kiddin'," Barton replied, as his confident smirk returned, as he added, "say, captain, maybe this would be a good time for me to ask for a raise."

"Yeah, well, as much as I'd like to talk to you about that, there's really no time."

"Ah, well, at least I can use the airline miles," Barton deadpanned.

"You're leaving first thing in the morning...United Airlines flight 1078. It departs at 7 a.m. out of O'Hare. You're booked in business class so you can get some rest while traveling, but get a good night's sleep tonight. You'll need it. Take a sleep aid if you have trouble sleeping in a chair because it's one helluva long flight."

Barton nodded.

"I haven't read many of the details," said Baskin, "but let me tell you, when you start reading through this, you're not gonna like it."

Chapter 1

Friday morning at 6:30 am Barton boarded a United Airlines flight at Chicago O'Hare's International terminal. It was the beginning of the longest trip of his life. Only once previously had he flown overseas when he and his wife, Sharon, flew to Europe for a vacation. But that flight to England would be nothing compared to what was ahead of him now.

Barton flung his carryon bag into the overhead compartment, settled his overweight six-foot, two inch two hundred thirty-pound frame into his seat, and reached for his seat belt as a flight attendant approached.

"Would you like some Champagne, sir?"

"Huh?"

The flight attendant smiled, "We serve complimentary Champagne in Business Class. Or if you prefer, we have orange juice."

Barton chuckled, thinking at this early hour it was much too early for anything alcoholic and that he'd probably get tipsy before he finished half a glass despite his size.

"Oh...uh...coffee please," he said.

"Certainly, sir, I'll get that for you right away."

About twenty minutes after takeoff Barton pulled the police file from his briefcase.

As he opened the folder, he wondered again if the Singapore Police had sent everything from their crime book by way of the American Embassy via diplomatic courier...wondered if they had copied every sheet of paper, every scrap of evidence.

Barton read the synopsis first and learned there had been four murders but what he saw next shocked him.

"Holy crap!" he said above the level of normal conversation.

"Sir?" asked the flight attendant startled, as she reached for his coffee cup to refill it.

"Huh? Oh...uh...excuse me. Sorry, it was nothing," he said, as Barton momentarily closed the file as she refilled his cup.

When the flight attendant moved on down the aisle, he reopened the file and re-read what had startled him. Each victim was a Singapore policeman!

No wonder the Prime Minister wanted to keep this quiet. Barton understood now why the Singapore authorities made quiet and unofficial inquiries to the U.S. Government as to whether Barton specifically was available to assist them. This would be an awful embarrassment to the Singapore government if it ever became public knowledge.

If the people of Singapore learned of this, it would freak them out. After all, if the police were targeted and they weren't safe, how vulnerable would the general public be? And if the killer suddenly switched targets from the police to civilians, there'd be nothing short of panic.

Barton wondered if the Singapore populous even had a hint of what was occurring.

"Probably not," he surmised. From what he'd read in the past about the Singapore government's propensity for keeping everything close to the vest, he doubted the government would be forthcoming with this kind of information. A leak of any kind would have immediately morphed into a full-blown frenzied news story.

Barton concluded that government pressure on the Singapore police to catch the killer must be enormous.

He continued to read and learned that each of the four victims had been stabbed in the front of the neck just below the voice box. Forensics determined that in each case the weapon was a knife with a serrated edge on one side.

"Up close and very personal," he thought.

Someone they knew?

Someone they trusted perhaps?

Barton took a sip of his coffee, and pondered the circumstances.

At the very least the killer had to be someone who could approach a policeman without arousing suspicion, without putting him on guard...someone a policeman wouldn't expect would do him harm.

That could happen once...twice maybe...but four murders in as many months after the police had been alerted?

Incredible!

Barton scribbled a note...*When could a policeman be taken unawares?*

In addition to the initial stab wound at the base of the throat, each victim had his throat slashed. The notes were very clear on the point that all four victims had their throats slashed from behind. That would make for far less splatter on the perpetrator Barton surmised, as he made another note...*frontal wound meant to stun victim.*

"*Hmm,*" thought Barton, "*why?*"

Barton scribbled: *Stab from the front; victims gasp for air; victims stunned; perpetrator moves swiftly behind and goes for kill.*

Barton continued writing.

Murderer moves very quickly...is very agile. The perpetrator is probably more agile than strong.

Barton read that the angle of the cut also identified the killer as right-handed. Barton paused to ponder that but almost as if he were incapable of concentrating on any other point, Barton kept coming back to the same aspect of the case.

How were the policemen approached?

Surely, after the initial two murders, the entire Singapore police force was placed on full alert for any suspicious looking character.

It just didn't make sense.

How had the latest two victims been approached as easily as the first two victims had been? How?

Barton continued reading. He reviewed every sheet of paper, the transcript of every interview, the details of each of the crimes, every line of information that had been delivered to Captain Baskin and he continued to jot notes as he read.

Before he knew it, the flight attendant was standing beside him. "Sir, we'll be landing in San Francisco soon; you'll need to fasten your seat beat."

"Oh, okay," he replied, as he fumbled for the seat belt.

As Barton closed the file, he wondered what facts may have been omitted. Invariably, some details were always overlooked, especially in what must have been a rush job to get the information copied and transported to the United States. Nothing was faxed. It was all hand carried.

Even though Singapore officials requested Lieutenant Barton by name to investigate the murders, he could be assured a few details might not have seemed important enough to a clerk who wished to finish the tedious chore of copying everything.

Barton would need to visit the police headquarters upon his arrival to be sure he reviewed all the information. It would be the only way for him to confirm nothing escaped his scrutiny.

In the meantime, Barton still had plenty of reading remaining and he would continue his examination of the facts once he landed in San Francisco, changed flights, and headed out over the Pacific on the next leg of his journey...toward Japan.

"Uh, Miss?" asked Barton, as the flight attendant moved back down the aisle.

"Yes, sir?" she replied politely.

"What time is it?"

"It is 9 am in San Francisco," she answered.

Barton sighed.

Singapore is fifteen hours ahead of San Francisco time so it was now midnight, Friday night, moving into Saturday morning in the Land of Orchids.

Chapter 2

At midnight in Singapore when Friday night moves into early Saturday morning, Orchard Road in Singapore is alive with a flurry of people and traffic. At first glance it appears fully half the population of the city has descended upon one of the city's most popular arteries as they eagerly usher in the weekend.

From the Compass Rose Restaurant & Bar high atop the 70th floor of the Westin Stamford Hotel, the lights of the city twinkle in the darkness as Singapore bustles with fast paced activity.

Down below on the main shopping district of Orchard Road what appear to be miniaturized automobiles clog one of the city's main thoroughfares. At street level the sound of tires screeching abruptly to avoid a fender-bender, and the inevitable blaring of horns fills the streets and numbs the ears.

Tourists and locals alike move briskly up and down the street shoulder to shoulder on the congested sidewalks. Shoppers quickly pop in and out of the many shops along the way as if afraid they might miss a bargain or a unique souvenir.

Seemingly leaping out of nowhere, a young man confronts a tourist with the words, "Copy watch!" He can furnish a tourist with a replica watch from a Piaget to an Oris, a Swiss watch to a Longines, while his most popular replicas remain a Rolex or an Omega.

"Copy watch," he repeats, until you wave him away.

Just off Orchard Avenue, a line extends down the sidewalk for nearly a block even at this late hour—-especially at this late hour on a Friday night—-of those awaiting entry into Singapore's Hard Rock Café.

While the locals generally take the inexpensive and clean modernized subway system into Singapore's main thoroughfare, the businessmen ride the more expensive taxis to their destination...all bumper to bumper as they flood Orchard Road with traffic.

Foreign visitors who are out for a good time and have a yearning for companionship merely veer off the main artery a couple of blocks to one of several night clubs in the area where they might meet someone to whom they are attracted. They will leave together and negotiate a price later, as they take taxi to a more secluded place for the fulfillment of their private desires and urges.

Amidst all the noise and congestion, among all the Singaporeans and tourists, the murderer walked slowly eastward down Orchard Road toward the Dynasty Hotel as some Singaporeans continue to refer to the hotel. Perhaps due to the British influence in the colonization of Singapore regarding most of the city's architecture, the Dynasty stands as an exception as a giant beacon of Asian influence in Singapore.

Among the swollen mass of Friday night fun seekers, the murderer was unnoticed and anonymous. At a stop light, the killer waited for the light to change, crossed the street at the corner of Orchard and Scott amidst the throng, and headed for the main entrance of the Dynasty Hotel.

The doorman at the Dynasty opened the door and nodded to the approaching pedestrian.

The killer smiled politely and walked casually through the entrance into the exquisite lobby. The walls are adorned with massive wooden panels that were intricately and meticulously carved by hand. In all, sixteen panels, eight on each of two different walls, extend from the floor up to twenty feet high toward the high ceiling. When fitted together, the carved panels tell of a legendary story in Chinese folklore.

When the Marriott chain took over the Dynasty Hotel to modernize the hotel, those beautiful, meticulously carved wooden panels were removed and a little more of the Chinese culture of Singapore was gone. Luckily, for visitors and locals alike, the panels were returned some years later to their rightful place in the city's proud panorama.

As the killer walked through the richly decorated lobby toward the elevator past the hand carved panels, a sick smirk flashed across the killer's face that slowly moved into a sadistic grin.

I carve quite well myself considering what I work with.

The killer approached the elevator and pressed the up button. The door opened, the killer entered and pressed five. There was no one else moving toward the elevator as the door closed.

The killer was alone.

When the elevator began its climb toward the fifth floor, in an odd custom of the killer's invention, the killer's eyes closed, raised a hand, and brought two fingers to the side of the head in concentration.

In mere moments, the killer smiled. All was well...just as planned.

When the elevator door opened on the fifth floor, the killer walked briskly down the hallway toward the stairway. There was no one on the stairwell as the killer quickly descended three floors, opened the door, and checked the hallway.

All was clear.

The killer moved into the second-floor hallway and moved quickly down the corridor toward the rest rooms at the end of the hallway. Just as the killer approached the men's washroom the door opened and a uniformed policeman entered the hallway.

A knife connected to a mechanism sprung from the killer's sleeve.

The killer lunged and thrust the knife into the policeman's throat below his Adam's apple.

The policeman staggered backwards as he gasped in pain. He attempted to raise his arms but couldn't as he was momentarily frozen, immobilized as the muscles in his body contracted and shook from the sudden shock of the intrusive blade.

Abruptly, the knife was pulled from his throat.

He gasped again.

Agonizing pain overtook him as he fought the inclination of falling as his knees were buckling.

In an instant the killer was behind him.

The sharp, serrated edge of the knife swept across the man's throat opening a large gash. Blood spurted profusely as both his jugular veins were severed.

Before the policeman fell to the floor, the killer was already moving swiftly away down the hallway.

A grotesque gurgling sound escaped from the policeman's throat. His arms flailed against the carpeted floor as his body convulsed and shook uncontrollably—-nature's death rattle.

The killer retracted the bloody blade out of sight back into a specially designed sleeve of padding and plastic to prevent any dripping or staining.

The killer moved briskly to the end of the hallway, turned left, and stepped onto the escalator which took the killer back down to the ground floor.

The killer crossed the lobby...not hurriedly but without delay...exited the Dynasty Hotel, and was back on Orchard Road in a matter of seconds.

In the anonymity and security of the crowd, the sadistic smile returned to the killer's face.

Chapter 3

Out over the Pacific, Barton continued his examination of the file, and a thought occurred to him. The killer knows the victims' every move! But as Barton continued to read, he saw his theory dashed.

The authorities were sure it wasn't anyone from the police force as every policeman was accounted for during the third murder...and the fourth. The killer was not a fellow Singaporean police officer!

"Maybe!" said Barton aloud, "maybe not. They could be wrong. After all, they haven't solved the case...that's why I'm heading there."

Barton continued his review of the facts. He was only about a third of the way through the file when he came across the information sheets on the victims.

Though not all four of the unfortunate victims had what could be interpreted as strictly Chinese surnames, Barton was struck by the fact that all four of them had westernized first names.

The victims were Mike Lu, Peter Ong, James Ing, and Robert Lee.

Whether the names were important or not remained to be seen but Barton noticed everything regarding a murder investigation.

Barton penned a note jotting down similarities between the victims in the hope of spotting something that would give him on a lead on the murderer or at least head him in the right direction.

Barton began.

All victims male, ages 23-29

When he noticed the flight attendant was coming down the aisle, he reached for his coffee cup, "Miss, I've finished here, if you could take this please."

"Certainly. Would you like anything else, sir?" she smiled politely.

"No thanks, I'm fine for now."

Barton pulled out the four information sheets and placed the manila folder on the empty seat next to him.

He always preferred the aisle seat whenever he flew so he was glad he got one. As it turned out, the flight wasn't sold out, so he was fortunate on this trip that the window seat wasn't occupied...at least from Chicago to Frisco and again now on the second leg of his journey over the Pacific. He had a lot of reading to do and he was very glad he didn't have some chatty individual seated next to him.

Barton spread the information sheets of the victims across the tray table, read one, then another, then another and the last one...his eyes scanning back and forth from sheet to sheet.

More notes followed...

All victims under 5' 7"

Barton noted each individual's height.

5' 6"

5' 6"

5' 5"

5' 4"

"Very short fellows," thought Barton, who was quite aware Asians are generally not as tall as Americans.

Barton paused for a moment to flip back through the papers in the file. It took a while to find what he was looking for...the coroner's report.

"Ah," he reacted as he located it again.

Barton looked for what he'd read earlier and found it. The angle of the cut across the throat was from behind...and very slightly downward.

Barton made another note.

Killer 5' 7" or 5' 8"

Barton re-read the part about the frontal wounds which the coroner stated had been the initial wounds in each case coming before their throats were cut.

One stab wound in throat

Barton shook his head as he looked again at the names of all four victims...Mike Lu, Peter Ong, James Ing, and Robert Lee.

He stared at their pictures and gazed into each set of eyes as they looked back at him.

Barton slammed his fist against the arm rest. Why?

After being convinced the first two cop killings weren't haphazard, why didn't the Singapore police require their patrolmen to wear high-collared flak jackets? Or at the very least why didn't they require high resistant plastic collars beneath their white ascots?

Why?

Slowly, Barton's anger turned to depression. It probably never occurred to them.

A high-resistant collar might have given the victims a chance. What a waste!

Barton wondered if they had families, people who missed them, as he closed the file and turned his attention back to the information sheets on the four victims and made more notes.

Mike Lu, single

Peter Ong, single

James Ing, single

Robert Lee, single

"Hmm," Barton rubbed his chin as he pondered the situation.

What kind of person would do such a thing to these men? He knew in his gut the fact that all the victims were single was not a coincidence, but that fact of and by itself wasn't necessarily important. He wondered if being single was significant or simply minutia of the case.

And then it hit him. Something very important was missing from the file.

Barton immediately reached for the in-flight phone and quickly dialed his home precinct.

"Ah, shit!" said Barton, "What's his extension? What is Crawford's extension?" yelled Barton, referring to his partner.

"Police Department," a voice answered. "May I help you?"

"Put me through to Sergeant Steve Crawford in homicide."

"Is there anything I can help you with?"

Barton recognized the voice of the officer at the front desk as that of Aloysius Parmeton, just as Aloysius recognized his voice.

"Is that you, Lieutenant Barton?"

"Yeah, Aloysius, there is something you can help me with."

"Oh, yes, sir, Lieutenant Barton. Anything at all," replied the desk Sergeant, who was always in awe of the renowned homicide detective. "Are you working on an important case? How can I help?" Parmeton asked, as he eagerly awaited an assignment connected with a homicide case being investigated by the famous detective. "What can I do, lieutenant? What can I do?"

Barton shook his head somewhere over the Pacific as the jetliner sped towards Japan.

"Aloysius...,"

"Yes, lieutenant, I'm ready to assist."

"You can put my call through to Sergeant Crawford; it's very important, Aloysius. Under no circumstances can I be disconnected."

There was a pause on the other end of the phone. "Oh," Aloysius replied, "Yes, right away, sir."

In a few moments, a voice answered, "Sergeant Crawford. May I help you?"

"Crawford!"

"Lieutenant, is that you?"

"Yeah, it's me. Guess my prodigy is really catching on. You're becoming quite a detective now. You're beginning to recognize voices. Gosh, you're almost as good as Aloysius."

"Oh, didn't you know, lieutenant?" said Crawford not skipping a beat. "He's my idol. Hey, by the way, where are you? You're supposed to be heading to Singapore."

"I'm over the Pacific now. There's nothin' but water below me."

"Oh. You know, as I recall, lieutenant, you have a bit of a phobia about driving on a bridge over water. How is that phobia when you're flying over an ocean?"

Barton hadn't thought about that thus far, and responded, "Thanks for that, Crawford."

"It's quite a case though, isn't it, lieutenant?"

"You know about it?"

"Yeah, I've been reading all about it."

"Huh?"

"Captain Baskin had a complete copy of the file made before he gave it to you. This morning he walks over to me with this three-inch file, throws it on my desk, and says, 'Here, Kid. Your partner Barton is working this case so read it. Knowing him, I'm sure he'll be calling you about something or other associated with the case sooner or later.'"

"Hmm," Barton mumbled.

"I've got to say, lieutenant, I didn't think you'd be contacting me this quickly."

"Well, since you're already familiar with the case, I've got a question for you, Crawford."

"Fire away."

"Have you seen a profile in that file?"

"A profile on the killer...uh...no, though I haven't read through the whole thing yet."

"Well, it doesn't matter. There isn't one."

"There's no profile at all? That's odd." Crawford mused.

"Yeah, I think so too. I need you to find out if the Singapore Police Department ever had a profile done on the murderer."

"No problem, I'll check it out with them right away. Is there anything else?"

"That's it for now."

"Uh, lieutenant," Crawford began.

"What?"

"If you have access to a phone, why don't you just make the call to the Singapore police directly?"

"Because Crawford, without me there in the Area office you don't have anyone to give you any assignments, and I don't want to hear you got bored. You know me. I've got your best interests at heart, Kid."

Crawford looked at the pile of papers on his desk pertaining to other cases, "Oh, yeah, lieutenant, nice of you to look out for me."

"Hey, if you doubt me, ask Sharon what a nice guy I am," said Barton, referring to his wife.

"You've forgotten. I've been over to your house a dozen times for dinner in the last year. I've talked to Sharon. I know what she thinks of the compassion you hold for your colleagues."

Barton chuckled, "Yeah, the real surprise is she still loves me. Anyway, I don't want anyone in Singapore knowing that I'm asking questions about them. It would be better if it comes from you...or better still...tell them Captain Baskin is asking since the file went through him."

"Okay, lieutenant."

"Start with the Singapore Embassy in the States. Light a fire under them and see what they can tell you."

"Will do," Crawford replied.

"I'll call you back in a couple of hours, Crawford, to see if you've come up with anything," said Barton, as he abruptly hung up and resumed his reading.

Chapter 4

Three more hours passed and all of Barton's meticulous reading was taking an effect. He paused and rubbed his eyes. He was weary. He gathered up the papers from the tray table, slid them back into the manila file. He needed to take a break.

Barton's stiff arthritic knees creaked as he arose. He walked up the aisle toward the bathroom and looked for the green unoccupied sign. Good, it was green and he entered. His six-foot, two-inch frame couldn't stand fully upright in the cramped restroom. "Well, if there's any turbulence, I certainly won't get bounced around in this sardine can," he mumbled.

He went to the sink and splashed some cold water on his face...and a lot more over his eyes. It felt very refreshing. After finishing, he exited the bathroom, and stood in the aisle for several minutes and stretched. Even in the expanded space of Business Class, his legs felt cramped and tightened from sitting so long. It felt good to stand up, stretch his legs and move around a bit. He realized he'd been sitting too long, so thoroughly involved in reading about the case.

Another man came out of the washroom on the opposite side of the aisle and Barton stepped aside to let him pass.

"Oh, I'm just gonna stand here and stretch my legs for a bit," he said so loudly that Barton immediately disliked the loud man, a fellow American.

"I'm in sales," he bellowed, as he extended his hand.

That figures, thought Barton, as he reluctantly extended his own hand.

"Hell of a flight, isn't it?"

Barton nodded, "Hmm."

"I'm heading to Japan. Ever been there?"

Barton shook his head.

"You'll love it. I've been to Japan lots of times...Japan, Korea, Taiwan. I'm heading for Japan now to nail down a sales contract with some Japanese businessmen. Hope to do pretty well. I've been told I can really back people to the wall...good negotiator. Are you going to Japan on business?" he bellowed so loudly Barton was sure those back in coach could hear him.

"I'm heading to Singapore."

"Ah, Singapore," the man repeated. "I've heard it's an enchanting land. Never been there myself. What's Singapore like?"

With a shrug of his shoulders, Barton gave the man the universal silent sign of...I don't know.

"Oh, first time there, hey?"

Barton nodded.

"Well, if Singaporeans are anything like the Japanese, Koreans, Taiwanese, they'll be very tiny...little people really...polite, but very short. Good workers though. Those little people can work from sun up to sun down...even work through lunch...and never slow down. Good workers; damn good workers. I remember this one time...,"

"Uh, excuse me," Barton interrupted, as he turned and headed back to his seat.

"Oh, well, good luck down there in Singapore," the man yelled after him.

What an asshole, Barton thought, as he walked away. No wonder so many Americans are thought of as obnoxious louts. Barton couldn't stand many of his fellow Americans either.

He glanced at his watch as he returned to his seat. It was past time to call Crawford in Chicago to see what he'd learned. Barton reached for the phone and dialed. As he was waiting for the connection, he let out an exasperating sigh. He'd forgotten to ask Crawford for his extension.

"Police Department, may I help you?" answered a voice on the other end of the phone.

"Hello, Aloysius," Barton deadpanned.

"Lieutenant, is that you again?"

"Yes, Aloysius, it's me."

"I saw Sergeant Crawford about thirty minutes ago and I told him you and I had spoken and that I'd offered to help in any way I can," he said proudly.

Barton paused as a smile crossed his face, and said, "I'm sure Sergeant Crawford was delighted to hear that, Aloysius."

"Would you like me to put your call through to him?"

"Yes, Aloysius, that would be very helpful."

"Right away, lieutenant, here you go."

There was a momentary pause. "Sergeant Crawford."

"Crawford. Barton. What did you learn?"

"Uh, yeah, I talked with the Embassy. We have the entire file, lieutenant. They don't have a profile on the murderer."

"You're kidding," said Barton.

"No. It seems since '65...,"

"65?"

"When Singapore became an independent country, well, they really haven't had any murders to speak of...and absolutely no serial killers. I doubt they even know what a profile is."

"Damn!"

"There is something else though. The Ambassador himself called me back less than an hour ago and told me to fill you in. There was another murder in Singapore earlier this evening. Sometime just after midnight Singapore time."

Barton's shoulders drooped, as he asked, "Another policeman?"

"Yeah, I'm afraid so...number five."

"Damn!" Barton yelled, as a couple of heads turned in his direction. "Frontal stabbing and throat cut?"

"Exactly," Crawford confirmed.

"And nobody saw anything again?"

"Right."

"Any other details?" Barton asked.

"Yeah, the Singapore police are posted in no less than pairs throughout the city...in some places even in threes."

"Was that the case before this latest killing?" Barton asked.

"Yeah, two officers were posted out in front of the Dynasty Hotel on Orchard Road. It's the busiest street in Singapore. It's got a lot shops, nightclubs, restaurants and the like. Anyway, one of the two officers stepped inside to go to the bathroom, and that's when it happened, in the hallway just as he came out of the bathroom."

"And no one saw it!!??"

"No. The bathrooms are up on the second floor...not off the lobby."

"Well, that does it," Barton declared.

"What, lieutenant?"

"It's not an inside job, Crawford. For a minute I thought it might be...even though the Singapore police had ruled that out. I thought they might be wrong and perhaps it was still a fellow cop committing all the murders, but no one is gonna have any inside information about when a cop is gonna take a whiz."

Sergeant Crawford nodded on the other end of the line. "Oh, there's something else," Crawford added.

"What?"

"The Ambassador wants you to call a Mr. uh...," said Crawford, as he searched for his note with a phone number, and continued as he found it, "a Mr. Jeffrey Ho in Singapore."

"Who's he?"

"Don't know, but the Ambassador wants you to call him immediately."

"You mean when I land in Singapore?"

"No, he wants you to call him right away."

"What's it about?"

"Don't know but that Ambassador was very clear that he wants you to call Mr. Ho from the plane a.s.a.p."

Barton glanced at his watch. "It's past two in the morning in Singapore, if I've calculated the time correctly."

The Ambassador said that Jeffrey Ho will be up expecting your call?"

Barton shrugged, "Okay. Give me the number."

As Barton wrote down the number, his curiosity peaked as he wondered what this was about and who Jeffrey Ho might be.

"Oh, by the way, lieutenant, though there wasn't any profile of the killer I asked the Ambassador and he said the files we received have everything, absolutely everything, down to the smallest scrap of paper from the Singapore police files. He said the Prime Minister insisted that everything, down to the last hand scrawled note, be sent to Chicago for your examination."

"Well, at least that's good to know, Crawford that we've got everything."

"Anything else you need?"

"Yeah, get a message to the Ambassador."

"What's that?"

"Tell him to get those boys in Singapore...everyone of 'em...an issue of protective collars."

Crawford nodded, "Yeah, I already did, lieutenant," said Crawford, as the two detectives disconnected.

Barton checked at his watch and did a quick calculation. He had figured wrong. He was off by an hour. It was now three o'clock in the morning in Singapore. He looked at the phone number that Crawford had given him...and the name of Jeffrey Ho.

Barton reached for the phone and placed the call.

"Hello?" a voice answered after one ring.

"Jeffrey Ho, please."

"Jeffrey here. Is this Lieutenant Barton?"

"Yes, I'm sorry about calling at this time...,"

"Not at all. I've been expecting your call."

"Why did you want me to get in touch with you?" Barton asked immediately.

"Do you know something about the case?"

"I was contacted by the Singapore Police to take a look into it and to put myself at your disposal?"

"Are you a police officer?"

"No."

"What then?"

"The authorities are not very experienced with serial killers. They have asked me to help you to develop a profile on the killer."

"You're a profiler, Mr. Ho?"

"Oh, please call me, Jeffrey, but to answer your question…I'm a profiler in a manner of speaking only. Anyway, I simply wanted to introduce myself and to let you know that I shall pick you up at the airport upon your arrival in Singapore. I have the connecting flight information on your flight from Japan."

"How will I recognize you?" Barton asked.

"The Singapore police department furnished me your picture they received from your Chicago office."

"I see."

"How are you coming in familiarizing yourself with the details?"

"I'm over half way through the file now."

"Then you shall have no problem in finishing before you land in Singapore," said Jeffrey, referring to the length of the journey Lt. Barton still had ahead of him.

"No. I'll certainly have plenty of time."

"Any thoughts thus far?" asked Jeffrey.

"Yeah…well…no…not exactly, just something that's bouncing around in my head that's bothering me."

"What's that, Lieutenant Barton?"

"How the killer so easily approaches the victims who are in fact police officers and are trained to be on their guard."

"I have thought long and hard about that too. Perhaps we shall see if you and I are on the same wavelength. Do you have a theory?"

"Not yet. We can discuss it tonight when I arrive."

"Until tonight then," said Jeffrey.

Chapter 5

Barton had closed his eyes on several occasions after he changed planes in Japan but was unable to fall asleep. When the rubber tires squealed against the runway in Singapore, he breathed a sigh of bone-weary relief.

"Finally!" he muttered.

It had been one hell of a trip!

At ten thousand miles away, there was only one way to get to Singapore...a horrendously long and tiresome full day of flying. His first junket was a four-hour flight to San Francisco, then one hour between flights before a ten-hour flight to Japan. In Japan, there was another wait of three hours before flying south for seven hours to Singapore.

A grueling twenty-five hours of traveling!!!

On top of that, he arrived in Singapore not at 8 a.m. Saturday morning—-twenty-five hours by the clock after he'd left Chicago—-but at nine o'clock Saturday night because of the thirteen-hour time difference.

Cy Barton's inability to sleep on airplanes had transformed him into a walking zombie by the time he arrived in Singapore, and he stood...barely stood...exhausted in the long immigration line at the Changi airport.

When the immigration officials opened another booth to check people through, a throng of travelers instantly rushed from in front of and behind Barton to form a new, shorter line. Barton stayed put. He was simply too tired to run into another line.

Because Barton was reviewing the case on the flight, he had not taken any pharmaceuticals to help him sleep and despite the fact he'd become exhausted and weary-eyed he didn't doze for even a few seconds. He discovered on his first overseas flight nearly halfway around the world that he simply could not sleep in a sitting position. He was just now beginning to feel the toll it takes on the human body.

Barton was absolutely bone tired as fatigue and exhaustion had set in and yet, unbeknownst to him at this point, were the effects of a thirteen-hour time change and jet lag that still lay ahead.

Luckily, the immigration line moved quickly and in ten minutes he was handing his passport to the official for examination, who stamped it. "Welcome to Singapore, Mr. Barton," said the official, as he handed Barton back his passport and immediately looked to the next person in line.

It was just as he had been briefed. There would be no special treatment for Barton so he wouldn't draw attention upon his arrival.

After clearing immigration, Barton went straight to the baggage claim and noticed immediately no bags had yet arrived on the carousel.

"That figures," Barton mumbled. "Why the hell should it be any different in Singapore than it is in the States? I wouldn't be surprised if they had the same damn union," he muttered.

Phase one on the flight from Chicago had already set in upon Barton from lack of sleep...extreme irritability.

While he was waiting for his bag, Barton saw a Bank of America sign and walked over. At least while he waited for his bag, he could exchange his U.S. dollars for Singapore dollars.

When he returned to the baggage carousel, he saw that other passengers on the flight were getting their bags, and he smiled to himself at his little shortcut of already converting his funds into the local currency.

Barton grabbed his bag and when he was waived through customs he continued and walked through the double doors to the main lobby.

Momentarily, a man approached him, and purposely did not address him by his official title, "Mr. Barton?"

"Jeffrey?"

"Yes. Welcome to Singapore," said Jeffrey, as he reached for Barton's suitcase.

"Thanks, but no need to do that," referring to his bag, as Barton felt uneasy that such a diminutive man would be carrying the burly detective's bag.

"It is my pleasure, Mr. Barton. My car is in the parking lot just across the street," said Jeffrey, as he led Barton out the doors.

A blast of hot, humid air immediately hit Barton in the face as he stepped outside. As Jeffrey and he walked across the pedestrian crossing toward the parking lot, Barton began to sweat profusely, and he quickly took off his coat and slung it over his arm.

"What a climate!"

Jeffrey commented, "It varies though...anywhere from eighty-five to ninety degrees everyday year 'round," he chuckled, "with a humidity anywhere from seventy-five to eighty percent."

"You mean it's always this humid in Singapore?"

"Every day, all year long, lieutenant," said Jeffrey, now feeling that it was safe to use Barton's official title as they were out of anyone's earshot.

"Singapore is only about sixty miles from the equator, you know."

He moaned, "Oh? I didn't know that. I suppose those of you who are from Singapore and live here all year long get used to it," said Barton, as he pulled out his handkerchief and wiped his forehead.

Jeffrey laughed loudly, "No one ever gets used to it," he chuckled, as he walked on.

"Here we are," said Jeffrey, but the car that Jeffrey Ho approached was a small Toyota Corona...a taxi cab.

Barton scratched his head, "You drive a taxi, Jeffrey?"

"Yes, this is my day job. I didn't pull into the taxi line because you didn't know I drive a cab and of course I wouldn't have been able to leave the car to look for you, so I just pulled into the parking lot here."

Barton continued to scratch his head as Jeffrey opened the trunk and stowed his bag and his carry-on, but kept his briefcase. He then made his way around to the right front door.

Jeffrey walked over, opened the door, and chuckled, "In Singapore, the steering wheel is on the opposite side of the car, lieutenant, the British influence you know."

"Oh," said Barton awkwardly, as he walked around the front and climbed in the other side almost stuffing his large frame into the front seat of the small Corona.

He felt not only cramped in the tiny car, but also very awkward while he was sitting in what would be the driver's seat on American cars, as Jeffrey pulled out of the parking lot and onto the highway.

As Jeffrey drove down the highway and moved into another lane, Barton grabbed for the missing steering wheel out of reflex each time the car veered slightly. It made Barton feel like he was out of control and careening toward certain death. Phase two kicking in on the long flight to Singapore...jumpy nerves.

The drive taken from the Changi airport to the hotels in downtown Singapore is the East Coast Parkway and Barton marveled at its scenic beauty. Though it was close to midnight, and only street lamps and automobile headlights illuminated the highway, the splendor of this tropical land was quite evident. An abundance of potted bushes and colorful, tropical flowers lined the paved median strip along the way, and countless large trees extended up, out, and over the highway from either side, which gave Barton the feeling that he was entering a forested tunnel. He looked to his left and saw the glow of hundreds of lights dotting the darkness from dozens of ships in the Singapore harbor. Only the Pacific Coast Highway in California he thought could compare to this scenic landscape. It gave him the impression he was entering a tropical paradise, which, Barton concluded, was exactly what Singapore was.

Jeffrey smiled. "Singapore is a lovely country, lieutenant."

"Indeed, it is. How big is the island?"

"Just two hundred and forty square miles," Jeffrey answered without hesitation.

"Very small," Barton mused..

"When this horrible matter of murder is finished, perhaps you will have some time to take in the sights of Singapore...Chinatown, Sentosa Island and its musical fountain, the Botanical Gardens where the National Orchid Garden within is said to have the most extensive display of orchids in the world. You must not miss your chance to see that...over 60,00 orchids over three hectares. That's about 7 ½ acres of them in your parlance. Singapore is called the Land of Orchids, you know."

"Yes, I believe I've heard that," Barton acknowledged.

"They grow wild here. It is the flower of our country; they are beautiful and they have a heavenly fragrance."

"Yeah," Barton nodded, as exhaustion from his trip overwhelmed him.

After several moments of observing his first exposure to Singapore, Barton turned to Jeffrey about something he had alluded to. "Tell me something, Jeffrey."

"Certainly, lieutenant, I am at your disposal."

"I don't get it. You drive a taxi. What do you have to do with the police?"

"The Singapore police contacted me for my assistance regarding a profile on the killer because I also have a bit of a reputation in another area."

"What is that exactly?"

"The Singapore Police keep me on a retainer. They pay me to continue to drive a taxi during the day, and I'm also allowed to keep whatever I make driving a taxi. They feel it's a wonderful cover. No one would suspect me of working for the police. It allows me to operate freely. I work for the police only at night as needed."

"But what is it that you do, exactly?"

"I'm a psychic," said Jeffrey, as he paused and eyed the lieutenant.

After several seconds, he stated, "You do not scoff at me with skepticism?"

Barton grinned, "A psychic was involved in a case I worked back in Chicago and was helpful. You might say I'm a semi-believer. I think it's improbable, but I do believe it's possible."

Jeffrey smiled. "I see. That is very open-minded of you. We shall work very well together, I should think, lieutenant, and I shall help you all I can to rid Singapore of this awful menace that has terrorized our peaceful land," said Jeffrey, as he pulled his taxi up in front of the Westin Stamford Hotel.

"Try to get a good night's sleep, lieutenant, and I shall meet you in the lobby in the morning. Is 7 a.m. okay?"

"That would be fine Jeffrey. 7 a.m. in the lobby."

Barton registered and took the elevator up to his room, but before he fell into bed he placed a call to the States.

"Hi, Hon," he said to Sharon, "I've arrived."

"How are you feeling?" asked Sharon.

"Like the living dead. I'm exhausted."

"I'll bet you are, but remember what I said. Be sure you get up early. You won't get acclimated to the time change if you sleep in."

"Don't worry. I already planned to meet someone for breakfast at seven."

"You have a good night's sleep," she said.

"Thanks. Love you," he said, as he disconnected.

Chapter 6

Before going to bed Barton ran a hot shower and after all those hours in the air it was the most soothing shower he'd ever taken in his life. He dried himself quickly when he got into bed he didn't so much go to sleep as much as passed out.

After a long overseas trip, the problem with jet lag isn't limited to being exhausted and adjusting to a new time zone. There's also the troublesome inconvenience of waking up in the middle of the night—-so totally wide awake there's no hope of ever getting back to sleep—-but it wasn't jet lag or the time change that bolted Barton upright in his bed at 3 am.

"Damn!" he yelled, as he fumbled for the light switch.

Barton jumped out of his bed, and, without so much as a glance at the clock radio on the nightstand, he crossed the room, went straight to his briefcase and pulled out the thick manila folder.

He scrambled through the many sheets of paper until he got to the photographs of the crime scenes. Of course, he didn't have any photographs of the fifth murder, which had occurred while he was over the Pacific, but he did have the photographs from the first four.

Barton spread the pictures out on the other twin bed in the room and meticulously examined the first set of photographs...nothing.

He spread the second set of photos onto the bed...carefully examining the area around the body but still nothing.

Then he spread out the photographs from the third murder, and there it was!

"Son of a bitch!" he shouted.

It was something he remembered seeing previously on the plane during his examination of the contents of the manila folder, but it hadn't registered in his brain until now when he suddenly awoke recalling what occurred at O'Hare in Chicago when he departed for Singapore and what Crawford had said.

Sergeant Crawford had picked Barton up at home and driven him to the airport. After Steve got the lieutenant's bag from the trunk, they were standing on the sidewalk at departures discussing a few things when someone approached them, "Got a light?"

"Afraid not," Barton had answered, just as Crawford reached into his pocket and pulled out a lighter and lit the man's cigarette.

"Thanks," said the stranger who then moved on.

"I've been working with you how long, Crawford? And I didn't even know you smoked," said Barton.

"I don't, lieutenant but hey...I'm single."

"Yeah, so?" Barton asked.

"Well, I just always want to be prepared to help, you know," Crawford grinned widely, "in case some tall, attractive lady needs a light."

Barton had simply shaken his head but now, as he looked at a picture of the crime scene of the third murder, he again said, "Damn!" as his eyes stared like a laser upon a cigarette lighter lying beside the body of a dead Singapore policeman, a cigarette lighter that the notes in the file said belonged to the victim.

"Son of a bitch!" said Barton, as he honed in on the gender of the killer.

Chapter 7

At seven o'clock sharp, Barton reached the lobby where Jeffrey Ho was already waiting for him.

"Hello, Jeffrey."

"Good morning, lieutenant. Did you sleep well?"

"Well, but not very long."

Jeffrey smiled, "Yeah, your body will take a while to adjust to the time change."

"Hmm," Barton muttered.

"A fine American breakfast will make you feel much better."

"Singapore has American breakfasts?" Barton asked in joyful anticipation.

"Yes, I thought you would prefer that."

"You bet I would!"

"This way then," said Jeffrey, as he led the Lieutenant out of the lobby and into Raffles City which not only houses the Westin Hotel, but also a large enclosed shopping mall connected to the hotel. At this early hour on a Sunday morning the mall was deserted, and it was only a short walk to an escalator that took them up to the second floor and the L'Express Restaurant.

"They serve an excellent American buffet breakfast," said Jeffrey as they entered.

Barton was famished because in Chicago it was actually 6 pm—-dinner time—-and his stomach was telling him as much, as it takes several days for the human body to acclimate itself to such a drastic time change. This would remain his normal dinner time for a few days and he would continue to awake with a ravenous appetite.

Immediately after they were seated a waiter came by with a large pot of coffee. Barton grabbed for his cup almost before the waiter was finished pouring, while Jeffrey asked for tea.

After the waiter moved on, Barton leaned toward Jeffrey, and asked, "What are the smoking laws in Singapore?"

"The smoking laws," Jeffrey repeated. "Well, one can smoke in their own residence or outside. Why? Do you smoke?"

"Me? Oh, no, I just wanted to know where a person is allowed to smoke in Singapore."

"There are appropriate and numerous receptacles throughout the city to dispose of the remnants of a cigarette, and, oh, there is a heavy fine for anyone casting a discarded cigarette butt on the ground."

"But that's it? Nowhere else?" Barton asked for confirmation.

"In no other buildings is anyone permitted to smoke...not even in bars any longer...and there are no longer any accommodations for smokers when they are at work."

When Barton's eyebrows arose questioningly, Jeffrey added, "There are no smoking rooms any longer within buildings. Smokers must go outside."

"Ah," Barton nodded. "That's why those policemen were so easily approached!"

"Huh?" said Jeffrey not understanding the lieutenant's point.

"The crime scene photos...one of the photos had a cigarette lighter beside one of the dead policemen."

"What do you make of that, lieutenant?"

"I'm still working on that," Barton replied, as he arose from his chair. "Well, if you will excuse me, Jeffrey, I'm going to see what they've got at the buffet. I'm starving."

Jeffrey nodded in understanding knowing that Lieutenant Barton's body was telling him it was dinner time. It would take a week for his body to acclimate to the time change, but as the lieutenant walked toward the buffet, Jeffrey's eyes appeared to glaze over into a distant stare.

Barton helped himself to bacon, eggs and toast and upon returning to the table, he immediately noticed Jeffrey's blank, trance-like stare. Unless Jeffrey was suddenly seriously ill, Barton knew from experience with a psychic what was happening, and he knew enough to remain silent while a psychic was concentrating.

When the waiter approached the table with the tea Jeffrey had ordered, Barton raised a forefinger to his pursed lips to be sure the waiter didn't disturb Jeffrey's concentration.

The waiter placed the tea quietly on the table and quickly departed.

As Barton sat silently watching Jeffrey Ho, he gobbled down some sausages and scrambled eggs all the while keeping his eyes fixed on Jeffrey and his trance-like state.

Suddenly, Jeffrey snapped out of it, and stated bluntly, "You're in danger, lieutenant."

"Me?"

"I didn't see it last night at the airport or when I dropped you off at the hotel. I didn't see it until now."

"What? What did you see?"

"A vision that you are in danger."

"Are you sure?"

"A psychic is never sure, lieutenant. We see things—-bits and pieces—-and we interpret those bits and pieces as best we can. Sometimes we interpret those clues correctly much like a detective interprets the clues of a case. The best psychics interpret what they see correctly more often than the less gifted psychics do."

"What did you see exactly?"

"Nothing that would make sense to anyone who isn't a psychic," Jeffrey explained. "It was an aura...an aura of danger."

Barton nodded and had a thought, "Is it true about psychics...that you can actually get quite tuned into someone if you touch something they've worn or something they've touched?"

"Not always, but yes, sometimes it helps," Jeffrey answered.

"Then we're gonna go somewhere and have you touch something the killer came in contact with."

"Where are we going, lieutenant?" as Jeffrey wondered what he would be touching.

"We're going to the morgue, Jeffrey, and you're going to examine the most recent murder victim from Friday night."

Chapter 8

Within the hour Jeffrey Ho stood hesitatingly over the cold, pale body of the fifth Singapore policeman to succumb to the killer.

As he hesitated, Barton noticed, and asked, "What's the matter?"

"They called me in on the case previously. I touched clothing that previous victims wore but I've never actually touched a dead person, lieutenant," Jeffrey answered, as he gulped in some air and swallowed hard. He appeared much more than simply nervous at the thought of doing so. He was downright frightened.

"And did you get anything from the clothing?"

"No."

"Then, all the more reason for you to actually touch the body," said Barton.

As the coroner handed the lieutenant a file containing his notes from the autopsy, Barton saw Jeffrey's anxiety. "We need your help, Jeffrey. Go ahead," he said as matter-of-factly as he could so as not to make a big deal out of it.

Tentatively, Jeffrey placed his hand on the head and face of the dead Singapore policeman and he was startled by its coldness and quickly pulled his hand away.

Jeffrey looked at Barton who nodded encouragement, and Jeffrey slowly placed his back upon the victim's face.

While Jeffrey tried to tune into the killer, Barton examined the notes of the fifth murder. The victim was David Tan, twenty-seven years old, five foot, six inches tall and single like the others.

After several minutes, Jeffrey turned and said, "I'm sorry lieutenant. I'm just not getting anything."

Barton saw the look of disappointment on Jeffrey's face, and said, "Don't worry about it, Jeffrey. It was just a thought and a long shot. Like you said...sometimes it works and sometimes it doesn't."

Just as they were about to leave, Barton got an idea. "Wait a minute!" he yelled, as he turned to the coroner, and said, "His clothes."

"What?"

"Where are this victim's clothes?"

The coroner nodded. "Just a moment," he said, as he left the room. The coroner returned with a bag of things and began laying them out on a table.

Barton turned to Jeffrey. "It's your normal mode of operandi so why not try again with these."

Jeffrey nodded as he approached and began to examine the victim's personal items...a watch, a ring, shoes, and clothing.

Suddenly, as Jeffrey picked up the victim's bloodstained shirt, the trance-like stare returned to his face.

Barton raised a finger to his pursed lips as he signaled the coroner for absolute quiet.

"Here," said Jeffrey, as he came out of his trance almost immediately.

"The killer held a hand here...upon his left shoulder...as the murderer stood behind the victim."

"Probably steadied the victim when cutting his throat," Barton surmised, as the coroner looked on in amazement.

"There wasn't anything else, Jeffrey?" Barton asked.

"Yes, there actually was something else that I picked up on, lieutenant," said Jeffrey with a look of grave concern on his face.

"What?"

"Not only does the killer know you're here, but it was the killer who arranged for you to be in Singapore."

Barton's eyes widened in silent incredulity as he stared at Jeffrey and all the facts of the case raced through his computer-like mind.

"Well, if you're right, Jeffrey, and you haven't misinterpreted something then you just gave us a huge clue."

Jeffrey smiled slightly but did not appear to understand clearly what the lieutenant meant.

"Come on," Barton urged him, "We're gonna go see someone."

"Who?"

"The man who sent for me," said Barton, as he looked at Jeffrey whose face showed the realization of who the lieutenant meant.

"We're going to see The Prime Minister," Barton continued, "and find out how he happened to personally request me."

Jeffrey's eyed widened as he had never met the Prime Minister.

"First, however, we're going to stop by the police headquarters," said Barton.

Chapter 9

Upon arrival at police headquarters, a uniformed officer led Jeffrey and the lieutenant into the office of Singapore's Chief of Police. As he arose to greet them, Barton saw a man of slight build at 5' 6" and probably no more than 150 pounds. Barton immediately deduced that the Chief of Police must work out regularly or he would have gained weight in his position behind a desk.

"Welcome to Singapore," greeted the Chief, as he shook, Barton's hand. "Thank you for coming so quickly, Lieutenant Barton. I trust you had a smooth flight."

"Smooth, yes, but very long."

"Oh, yes. We are a long way from Chicago. No doubt it is a very tedious flight. I just wish you were visiting our land under better circumstances."

"Perhaps when this is over," Barton offered.

"Yes, perhaps," the Police Chief nodded. "I certainly hope you can help us with this, and I think you have quite a good assistant," he said, as he turned and toward Jeffrey and extended his hand.

"Though you occasionally work undercover, I am aware of your reputation, Mr. Ho. It is my pleasure to meet you."

Jeffrey glowed with pride but said nothing in return as he was caught speechless.

The Chief of Police glanced toward Lt. Barton, and explained, "Jeffrey is quite a psychic...not with the general public at large in Singapore mind you, as that would blow his cover. But I am keenly aware of his gift. He has assisted us on several cases in the past. I think Jeffrey could very well be of help to you in this investigation."

Jeffrey felt an overwhelming pride swelling within him and hoped he could live up to what the Chief was saying.

"I think so too," Barton replied while Jeffrey nodded in appreciation while still speechless.

"You are familiar with the contributions that a psychic can make to a police investigation?" the chief asked. "Have you had some experience with psychics in your country, Lieutenant Barton?"

"A little."

"Well, I must say, you have quite a reputation yourself. You are a very renowned detective. The Prime Minister asked for you personally, you know."

"Yes, that's my understanding. What can you tell us about that specifically?"

"What do you mean?"

"How did the Prime Minister happen to ask for me?" Barton inquired.

"Well, I received a call from him a few days ago. He asked me about you. I, of course, was familiar with your prowess on homicide investigations as so many of us are familiar with one another around the globe in this business and I told him what I knew."

"So, he was already aware of me when he contacted you."

"Yes, as I stated, he asked about you by name."

"Did that seem a bit odd to you?"

"Odd?" he repeated the question.

Barton rephrased his question. "Did it seem to you a bit unusual that I was known to the Prime Minister...that he was aware of my work?"

"As a matter of fact, it did surprise me a bit when he said he was familiar with your work. I mean, he deals in politics, not crime, but as we spoke, I got the feeling I was merely confirming to him what he already knew."

"Was there anything you said about me that you felt he didn't know?"

"Without hesitation the Police Chief replied, "No."

"Hmm," said Barton, as he glanced at Jeffrey who smiled slyly. "What is it, Jeffrey?"

"I was simply thinking that one need not be a psychic to see there are wheels turning in your mind lieutenant."

Barton chuckled.

The wheels in his detective's mind were indeed turning as Barton thought the situation might be quite the opposite of what the Chief of Police surmised. To Barton it sounded like the Prime Minister might not know anything about Barton...that someone else informed him about the homicide detective, and the Prime Minister was seeking confirmation of what he heard. It was something politicians often did in the States and Barton thought it might be a universal trait.

Barton smiled, "I think Jeffrey and I should meet with the Prime Minister. Is that something you can arrange."

"Certainly," said the Chief of Police, as he reached for the telephone. "I'll make a call for you to be placed on the Prime Minister's calendar this afternoon."

"Thanks, I appreciate that."

The Police Chief then arose from his chair, walked from behind his desk, approached, and said, "We have nearly a hundred men working on this, and though I have the utmost respect for their competence, I want you to know I was not offended when the Prime Minister suggested you. As I said, we have heard about you, and we can use all the help we can get from your expertise."

"I appreciate you saying that, Chief, and from my examination of the file I could see that your department was very thorough," Barton made a point of returning a compliment and went on to specify what he meant. "The file showed that all former rejected police applicants...going back as far as five years...were investigated thoroughly, and that all of them were cleared. I also saw that all former Singapore police officers who were dismissed due to misjudgments, malfeasance, incompetence, or corruption were also investigated which covered those with a possible grudge against the Singapore Police force."

"Yes, but unfortunately all of that hard work did not give us a single lead on who the killer might be."

"But it all helps, Chief. At least we know who the killer isn't and that will make my job easier since your department has eliminated so many."

"Oh, uh, one thing I should point out, lieutenant," said the Chief.

"What's that?"

"As you proceed in the case, everything you learn must be passed to this office...to me specifically...and to the task force. I hope you understand."

"I most certainly do and that's not a problem," Barton agreed, "I'll update you every day with what I learn about the case," as he shook the Chief's hand.

"Good luck to you then," said the Chief and added, "By the way, did you bring a fire arm with you?"

"I did not."

"Then we shall issue you one as well as Singapore police credentials so that you will have jurisdictional authority. Pick them up on your way out," said the Chief, as he scribbled a note. "Here, just give this to the desk sergeant," as he handed it to Barton.

After Barton was issued the weapon and they exited Police Headquarters, Jeffrey said, "If the Police Chief is correct, it sounds like the Prime Minister was being a careful politician and checking things out before acting on information that he might have heard unofficially."

"Very tactful, Jeffrey," Barton grinned.

"Do you think it could be someone on the Prime Minister's staff?" asked Jeffrey.

"Perhaps," mused Barton, "and if your psychic ability is correct that the killer arranged for me to be in Singapore, then, if not on his staff, it's certainly someone who has the Prime Minister's ear, and someone whose opinion he trusts to some extent. If not, the Prime Minister would never have sent for me," said Barton, as he approached Jeffrey's taxi and once again found himself standing on the driver's side of the car. Barton shook his head and grunted as he repeated his mistake of last night and walked around the car to the passenger's seat and got in.

Chapter 10

It was 3:30 in the afternoon when Barton and Jeffrey took a seat in the waiting room of the Prime Minister's living quarters. The Prime Minister agreed to meet them at his residence since he would not be in his office in the Parliament building on a Sunday afternoon.

Barton leaned in and whispered, "Keep those sensory receptors of yours wide open, Jeffrey. You never know what you might pick up."

Jeffrey's face suddenly showed a bit of nervousness.

"If you would, this way gentlemen," said the house butler from the doorway.

Barton and Jeffrey arose and followed the butler down the hallway and into a small library. The Prime Minister was seated behind a desk.

"Come in gentlemen, come in," he greeted them.

"Thank you for seeing us in your home, Mr. Prime Minister," said Barton.

"No problem, no problem. I never go into the office on a Sunday."

Barton formally introduced himself as well as Jeffrey who stood in awe of his country's Prime Minister.

Barton reached into his coat pocket to pull out his badge, but the Prime Minister stopped him. "No need for that Lieutenant Barton. I have seen your picture, and of course I am familiar with your reputation as renowned detective. Afterall, that's why I requested you. I am also quite aware of Mr. Ho's superlative assistance in working with our Police force," the Prime Minister nodded in Jeffrey's direction.

Jeffrey was once again flattered.

Sit, please sit, gentlemen," he urged them, as the Prime Minister motioned toward a couple of eighteenth-century high-backed chairs in front of the desk.

As they took a seat the Prime Minister said, "Though it is Sunday, I do a lot of work from my office here, so I shall come right to the point. It's a terrible situation we find ourselves in here in Singapore...just terrible. Are you fully briefed on the case, lieutenant?"

"Yes, I have reviewed the entire file on the flight over the Pacific. Thank you for arranging to have everything copied and sent to Chicago before I departed for Singapore. It was quite a time saver and the file was quite thorough."

"Good, good. Yes, I figured that would be best with all the time you'd have in the air during such a trip. It is a terribly long flight, isn't it? I have been to the States several times and it is never enjoyable...the flight I mean. Of course, I have it a bit better than you with a private jetliner equipped with a bedroom and all. I hope you understand why we didn't make that available to you, lieutenant."

"I understand fully, and may I say that I agree with you in keeping my presence low key."

"Good," the Primed Minister nodded.

"I am curious though, Mr. Prime Minister. How is it that you happened to request my assistance? I mean, as opposed to any number of other fine detectives throughout the world who are just as good not to mention those in your own police force."

"You are too modest Lieutenant Barton but I understand your curiosity. I must admit to you that it wasn't me who thought to request your assistance. It was a member of my staff. You see, any public official is only as good as his or her staff."

"And who on your staff mentioned me to you...if you don't mind me asking."

"Ah, the detective in you, Lieutenant Barton. Asking questions is in your genes," the Prime Minister chuckled.

Barton nodded as in confirmation to what the Prime Minister stated.

"To answer your question, it was one of my advisors, Catherine Lim, who recommended you and brought your expertise as a detective to my attention. My only regret is that I didn't act on her recommendation sooner. Perhaps you will meet her during your stay here. She is one of my most trusted advisers...very competent, quite intelligent, and very lovely if I may say so."

"Perhaps I'll have a chance later to thank her for recommending me. It's nice to know that I am so well thought of in your country."

The Prime Minister nodded.

"We'll do our very best not to let you down, Mr. Prime Minister, and do everything we can to find this killer as quickly as possible."

"My entire staff and all the resources of Singapore are at your disposal, Lieutenant."

"Thank you. I appreciate that, Mr. Prime Minister," said Barton, as he arose to shake his hand.

"Good luck then, gentlemen," he said, as he also shook Jeffrey's hand, "and do keep me posted on your progress."

"Of course, Sir," said Barton, as Jeffrey nodded in agreement.

As they departed the Prime Minister's residence, Jeffrey asked, "So, did you have a favorable impression of our Prime Minister, lieutenant?"

"Well, I'd say there's not too many politicians in my country who ever give their staff much credit—-for anything—-even in private conversation. I know because I've talked to plenty of them over the years in my line of work. Your Prime Minister sounds like a very honest man, Jeffrey."

"Yes, I admire him very much and he is well respected in our country."

"Yes, I've heard that he is quite popular here."

Jeffrey nodded his acknowledgement.

"How about you, Jeffrey. Any impressions from our discussion with the Prime Minister? Did you receive any signals?"

Jeffrey shook his head, and said, "I am afraid not."

"Well, perhaps there just wasn't anything there for you to pick up on, or maybe you have just cleared the Prime Minister of murder," Barton grinned.

Jeffrey laughed robustly.

"So where do we go from here, lieutenant?"

"Let's head back to my hotel."

"Are you tired, lieutenant?"

Barton smiled weakly, as he replied, "Damn right I'm tired. I feel like I'm about ready to tip over."

"It's the jet lag kicking in but you mustn't nap. You need to stay awake to overcome it."

"No, I wasn't planning on any nap. This case will keep me alert enough but I sure could use a cool drink about now. Let's go. I'll buy you a drink at the hotel bar."

As they headed back toward the hotel, Barton reached for his cell phone and called the Police Chief.

"Chief, I'd like you to get me everything you can on a Catherine Lim, but keep it very quiet. She works for the Prime Minister."

"Is she a possible lead, lieutenant?"

"Don't know yet, but I want to know everything about her...her history, where she lives, where she goes, her friends, her associates, her height and weight, absolutely everything, even down to what she eats for breakfast."

"We'll get on it immediately and I'll call you when we've got something."

"Thanks, Chief, but please gather everything very discreetly, since she is on the Prime Minister's staff," Barton emphasized again.

"That goes without saying," said the Chief, as Barton felt a bit embarrassed, and hoped he hadn't sounded patronizing.

Hearing Barton's side of his conversation with the Chief of Police, Jeffrey said, "I know Catherine Lim."

Barton did a slow turn toward Jeffrey, and asked, "Do you know her well enough to set up a meeting?"

"I have spoken with Ms. Lim on a couple of occasions so I can arrange that, yes, if you wish to speak with her, I know where her office is and...,"

"Oh, I wish to speak with her," Barton echoed enthusiastically, "but outside of her office...privately without raising suspicion and don't let on why I wish to speak with her."

"Not a problem, lieutenant."

Chapter 11

Barton sat down at a secluded table against a back wall in the hotel bar. He was confident that he could have a conversation with Catherine Lim here without anyone overhearing them...at least for now while there were few people in the bar area before the late afternoon rush.

The information gathered on Catherine Lim had been very thorough indeed. Well educated and extremely bright, Catherine Lim entered the Singapore civil service and exceled. Now, at thirty-four years of age, she was a rising star in the Singapore government. She moved up rapidly through the State department and became a member of the Prime Minister's cabinet, and it was said she would one day be an excellent candidate for Prime Minister herself. She was so devoted to her career that she had not married and only recently had become engaged...to another member of the cabinet.

A female at t 5' 7" Catherine Lim fit the profile of the killer Barton had developed, and of course it was Catherine Lim who had recommended to the Prime Minister that Lieutenant Barton be called in on the case.

When a waitress approached, Barton ordered a diet Pepsi, as he waited patiently for Catherine Lim, while Jeffrey was in the hotel lobby as he awaited Catherine's arrival. Barton had instructed Jeffrey not to divulge anything about their conversation with the Prime Minister, but to merely state Barton was here from Chicago and he wanted to meet the person who recommended him to the Prime Minister.

When Jeffrey saw Catherine enter, he immediately approached.

"Catherine, it is good to see you again. You're as lovely as ever," he said, as they shook hands.

"Thank you and you certainly look well, Jeffrey."

"I try to stay in shape, thanks. I need to make several phone calls, but this way," he gestured with his hand, "and I shall introduce you to Lieutenant Barton from Chicago."

Barton saw Jeffrey and Catherine Lim approaching and arose from his chair, "Catherine Lim, I assume."

"Yes," she said, extending her hand.

"Lieutenant Barton. It is nice to meet you."

"And you as well."

"Well, I need to make some phone calls," Jeffrey stated, "if you'll excuse me."

"Yes, of course," said Catherine.

Barton nodded toward his Singaporean partner, as Jeffrey bowed ever so slightly to them both and departed.

Please, sit down," Barton gestured toward a chair. "Would you like a cool drink?" he asked, as he gestured for a waitress.

"Thank you, yes. Here in Singapore a cool drink is always appreciated."

When the waitress approached, Catherine said, "I'd like a glass of cranberry juice please."

"Yes, ma'am. I'll be right back with that."

Catherine turned toward Barton, and said, "I am somewhat surprised."

"Oh?"

"Yes. I didn't even know the Prime Minister acted on my suggestion."

"Yes, well, we agreed it was best to keep my involvement confidential."

"Then I don't understand why you...," Catherine paused, as the waitress brought her cranberry juice, set a coaster on the table, placed the drink upon it, and immediately left.

As soon as the waitress was gone, Lt. Barton began a conversation with Catherine that went on for the next twenty minutes.

When Jeffrey had stepped away, he stayed within sight of their table and was on his cell phone when he saw Catherine arise and exit the hotel.

"Okay, I have to go," said Jeffrey, who added to his wife, "love you. See you later." He disconnected and proceeded immediately to see if Lt. Barton had learned anything from his discussion with Catherine Lim.

As Jeffrey sat down, he asked, "How did it go, lieutenant?"

"It went quite well. I learned a great deal, Jeffrey. I'll tell you my thoughts over dinner."

"It's not even five o'clock yet," Jeffrey pointed out.

"That's all right. We've things to discuss over another cool drink. If you don't mind us not going with the local cuisine, are there any Italian restaurants in Singapore?"

Chapter 12

"I am actually glad you had a taste for Italian, lieutenant, as I was just telling my wife that we should go out for Italian when I am off this case."

"Oh, sorry, if I ruined...,"

"Oh, no problem at all. I can go twice," Jeffrey chuckled.

Barton nodded, "Of course."

As they got into a taxi, Jeffrey said, "Nice to ride in someone else's taxi for a change."

"I'll bet it is," Barton agreed, "you don't have to mess with traffic."

Jeffrey told the driver, "Take us where the East Coast Road becomes Mountbatten Road, the Volare restaurant."

The driver nodded in acknowledgement, "Yes, sir."

When they arrived at the Volare, it was crowded but Jeffrey was able to get a table for two without a reservation as he had called ahead.

"I know the owner."

Barton grinned, "Just like in the States...it's nice to know people."

"I hope you will like this place. My wife, Jeanne, and I have been here and we like it."

"I'm sure it will be fine."

After each of them had ordered another cool drink, they spoke in hushed whispers as the tables were not far apart.

"If I am correct, we are dealing with a very different kind of serial killer," Barton stated.

"How do you mean?"

"Well, killers have motives, some kind of motive. That gives the police something to go on, and most murderers that are caught are arrested within 12-16 hours of the crime. After about four days, the odds of closing a murder case become higher and higher. But serial killers for the most part don't have a motive in the sense that other murderers do. That's what makes them so difficult to catch. They kill for the thrill of it...for the hunt...for the high it gives them, and the more they kill...the more they want to kill. Killing for the sake of killing is their motive. Generally, they go after those who are vulnerable...women, the elderly. Prostitutes are one of the most common targets...at least in the States anyway."

"Why is that," Jeffrey asked

"Because prostitutes are so easily approachable."

"Ah," Jeffrey acknowledged.

"But in this case, the killer is targeting the police. I've never heard of a case like this before anywhere in the world. It's the one group of people that would be the least vulnerable. They're trained to be alert and on guard and they're armed. And this killer isn't killing to get some kind of sick high."

"What do you mean, lieutenant?"

"This killer has a reason...a motive unlike any serial killer I have ever heard of or studied."

"Do you have a lot of serial killers in the States?" Jeffrey wondered.

"Sadly, yes, and the estimates are that there are anywhere from 40 to 50 serial killers operating at any given time in my country."

"Oh, my God," Jeffrey shuddered. "I can't imagine what that must be like."

"Yeah, it's pretty sick," said Barton.

The waiter came with their drinks, and placed them on the table. "Would you like to order now gentlemen?

"Uh, no," Barton replied quickly. "We have business to discuss but we will get your attention when we are ready."

"Very good, sir," the waiter nodded and left.

Barton then noticed Jeffrey looking away, as if avoiding eye contact. "What is it? Are you picking up on something?"

Jeffrey appeared somewhat embarrassed, as he replied, "There is something I didn't tell you."

Barton shot him an icy stare. "Oh? What's that?"

"Well, it was back at the morgue. I picked up on something...I mean...I think I did. I didn't keep it from you intentionally. It's just that I wasn't sure, you know, of its meaning, whether I interpreted it correctly or not."

"You can't hold anything back, Jeffrey. Since we are working together, I've got to know everything you and your sixth sense detect...right or wrong. Otherwise, it wouldn't make much sense for me to work with a psychic, would it?"

"I guess not. You are right. I apologize...uh...,"

"There's no need to apologize," said Barton, as he lifted his glass, nodded in Jeffrey's direction and took a sip while Jeffrey took a long gulp of his.

"So, what is it you didn't tell me?"

"Well, I'm not positive, mind you, but I think the killer might also be a psychic."

"Son of a bitch!" yelled Barton, as he slapped the table a bit more loudly than he intended as heads turned at nearby tables in his direction.

Barton mouthed the word, *sorry*, to those around him and then contemplated what Jeffrey had said. As the wheels turned in his mind, he reflected on that possibility, and Barton nodded repeatedly with a gleam in his eyes.

"Like I said, I'm not really sure, but...," Jeffrey paused as he was taken aback, and not quite understanding the lieutenant's demeanor, as he asked, "You are happy about this possibility?"

"Don't you see?" said Barton in a muted whisper. "That makes a lot of sense. That's how the killer would know when the victims were alone...even if only for a few seconds...and appear at the scene at precisely the right moment," Barton surmised.

"Or be at the scene waiting until the killer's psychic ability kicked in and indicated when the next victim would be vulnerable," Jeffrey offered and then repeated his earlier warning, "You are in danger, lieutenant."

"Yeah, you mentioned that," said Barton, in a manner brushing off the warning.

"It is a very strong feeling, and that feeling has been getting stronger which I interpret to mean the killer will move against you soon."

Barton raised an eyebrow, and asked, "How soon?"

"I can only interpret by how strong the feeling is. From that I can determine a time frame. The feeling is stronger than it was before," Jeffrey repeated, "so I believe it will be sooner rather than later. I think within days...perhaps sooner."

"I'm not sure anymore with the International Date Line I crossed," said Barton, as he asked, "What's today's date?"

"It's August 30th. Why?"

"Well, that's going to put us into September, a new month."

Not quite understanding the lieutenant's point, Jeffrey shook his head, "Is that of significance?"

"Though the number of days between killings has no apparent pattern, the killer has struck for the last five consecutive months."

"Oh, how could I have missed that?! That is so obvious!" Jeffrey admonished himself, and, as he thought about the lieutenant, he became very depressed.

"Hey! Don't look so down, Jeffrey. The killer hasn't gotten to me yet," Barton smiled slyly.

Jeffrey's eyebrows arose as a thought struck him. "I might be able to help you."

"How is that?" Barton asked, as he took another sip of his Pepsi.

"Maybe we can trick the killer."

"If the killer is as good a psychic as you apparently believe, how might we do that?"

"If the killer is tuned into you, as well as the Singapore police, then I would have free reign," Jeffrey noted.

Barton paused to consider what Jeffrey said.

"A bit devious. I like that. It's a good quality to have if you ever wished to go into police work full time," Barton commented, as he took another sip of his Pepsi, set his glass down, and asked, "but if we can think of a plan, and develop it, discuss it, won't the psychic killer become aware of it?"

"Not if I don't tell you," Jeffrey stated, as now it was his turn to smile slyly.

"No," Barton shook his head decidedly, "it's too dangerous. Besides, you're a civilian. I couldn't allow it."

"I'm your assistant, lieutenant. Besides, as you already know, I work for the police."

"Not in the capacity of a law enforcement officer," Barton differed.

Barton looked long and hard at Jeffrey Ho and his Asian partner repeated what he'd said before, "It is not me who is in danger, lieutenant. It is you."

Barton continued to eye his new friend, and asked, "Before I can make a definitive statement, I'll need to know exactly what you have in mind. You see, I don't have your intuitive powers of perception. You'll actually have to spell it out for me."

"That's the whole point. I can't tell you, because that would risk the killer possibly learning of my plan."

Barton rubbed his chin while pondering Jeffrey's proposal.

Finally, he pulled out his phone, "Okay, but not for a few days. I have an idea of my own," he said, as he dialed a phone number in California where it was now 4 am.

A groggy, sleepy voice answered and moaned into the phone, "Hmm."

"Pete. This is Barton."

Barton abruptly pulled his phone away from his ear, because of the shouting on the other end of the line.

"Yeah, yeah, I know what time it is," said Barton. "I need a favor. I need you to get your ass out here, tomorrow!"

"I'm working this week. I can't just...,"

"Call in sick. It's important."

"Dammit!" Pete yelled. "I'll never know why I do these things for you every time you call," as he swung his feet out from under the covers and onto the floor.

"Here's what we need," said Barton, as he went on to specify what he needed from Pete.

"All right, all right," Pete agreed reluctantly, and asked, "Where is it, this time? Are you in Chicago or one of the burbs?"

Barton pulled the phone away from his ear and grimaced in anticipation of Pete's reaction, as he answered, "I'm in Singapore."

Chapter 13

Two nights later, when Pete's plane touched down in Singapore, Lieutenant Barton and Jeffrey Ho were there at Changi airport to pick him up. After Pete exited the plane and went through immigration, he was so tired from the grueling flight he could barely stand.

With a carry-on bag only for his proposed short stint in Singapore, Pete went straight to customs and cleared without incident.

Pete passed through the doors and into an open area where dozens of people awaited. Some were family or friends of the arriving passengers while others were hired drivers, holding signs with the names of those they were to pick up.

When Barton saw Pete, he commented, "Pete better be careful or they'll arrest him for suspected drug use regardless of having cleared customs the way he is wobbling," though having recently experienced the hideous flight, fully understood how Pete felt.

Jeffrey was holding a sign with his rider's name as Pete approached, and said, "So, my supposed friend, Barton, was too cowardly to pick me up himself."

Jeffrey merely replied, "This way, sir."

When they go to Jeffrey's car, Barton six-foot, two-inch frame was scrunched in the back as Pete got in the front and found himself behind the wheel.

"Other side," Barton smirked from the back seat, as Pete got out and walked around to the passenger's side and got in there, as Jeffrey got in behind the wheel.

"You're a son of a bitch, Cy Barton!"

Barton let the chide go unanswered. "I booked you a room at the Dynasty where I'm staying and we'll go there directly so you can have a good night's sleep. You to be fully rested because we need you to do your best work."

Jeffrey pulled out of the parking garage and headed for the hotel.

"You're going to wake up famished," Barton informed him, "so we'll meet you at eight o'clock sharp in the lobby and we'll take you for a hardy American breakfast. I'll fill you in then on what we need you to do."

"Hmm," was all that Pete could utter as his eyelids drooped and he was now slumped as he leaned against the car door.

Chapter 14

The next morning after breakfast at the L'Express Restaurant, Pete declared, "Oh, that hit the spot!"

"I thought you'd like it," said Barton, as he turned toward Jeffrey and grinned.

"Yeah, and you weren't kidding. I was starving!"

"Yeah, we figured you would be," Barton chuckled, "and breakfast is on me."

"I would hope so after making me come this far."

"So, are you ready to get to work?"

"Yeah, that's why I brought my kit down."

"And you remembered to pack what I requested?"

"Yep."

"Okay, then. We shall head back to the hotel and you can get started."

Pete was meticulous and it was several hours later before he finished. Pete stepped back and examined his latest endeavor. He took pride in his work and he smiled within himself at another job well done.

Barton now made a thorough examination of Pete's labors, nodded repeatedly, and commented, "Yeah, I think that ought to do it. You're the best, Pete."

"You're damn right I'm the best!"

"Damn!" Barton yelled. "We've got to get to the airport! Pete's flight!"

Pete scowled at the thought of getting on a plane so soon after his arrival in Singapore.

Pete grabbed his carry-on and it was late in the afternoon when Jeffrey pulled to a stop for departures at the Changi airport.

"I don't envy you the long, grueling flight home so soon," said Barton.

Pete wasn't crazy about it either, as he responded, "You're a son of a bitch, Barton."

Again, Barton did not retort to a rebuke from Pete, but said, "Your flight back to California has a four-hour stopover in Tokyo, so peruse the duty-free shops and try to relax."

Pete glared at Barton, as he said, "I hope I don't hear from you for the next decade."

Invariably, Pete knew he would hear from Barton again one day...most probably sooner rather than later. Barton would ask for his expertise again and Pete would moan; and he'd complain; but in the end he would relent and do what his good friend requested, because whenever his friend Barton needed help, Pete was never able to refuse.

Chapter 15

For the next two days, Barton spent his time going back and forth from Police Headquarters and continually reviewed every detail of the case, but ever since Jeffrey warned Barton of the impending danger, the lieutenant was on the alert every waking moment.

On Thursday morning at 7 a.m. Barton walked across the deserted mall of Raffles City on his way to the L'Express for another American buffet breakfast. Jeffrey was not with him this morning, as he had informed Barton that he had an early appointment on personal business that he could not cancel.

Unbeknownst to Barton, the killer lay in wait out of sight.

Though the killer could not physically see Barton, the sixth sense of psychic ability honed in on him. "*All clear*," the killer thought, as a sick, sadistic smile began to form.

At this time of morning there was no one else on the ground floor of the mall because other than the restaurant, the shops were not yet open. Barton was alone and he was unaware that he was about to come face to face with the murderer.

This was the moment the killer had waited for and the killer's anticipation and eagerness mounted as the famous homicide lieutenant approached.

At precisely the right moment, the killer began walking...slowly.

Suddenly, as Barton turned a corner, he was startled as a tall woman approached him.

"Excuse me," she said holding a cigarette in her left hand. "May I trouble you for a light?"

Barton reacted immediately and reached inside his suit coat but he wasn't reaching for a cigarette lighter.

Suddenly, the woman lunged toward him...a large, serrated metal blade protruding from her sleeve.

In that split second, Jeffrey Ho appeared out of nowhere and leapt between Barton and the killer.

Barton fell backwards to the floor as the knife caught Jeffrey in the chest but didn't penetrate. The would-be assassin knew immediately the leaping intruder was wearing a protective vest so the killer slashed the blade wildly across Jeffrey's throat. Blood gushed forward and splashed onto the killer as this time she was in was in front of her victim.

Jeffrey's knees wobbled and he fell to the ground…his blood spurting onto the tile floor.

The killer slipped momentarily in the blood but recovered quickly and in an instant was gone as she raced away.

Barton unhurt scrambled to his feet and ran after her.

In an empty mall, the killer did not have the luxury of blending into the anonymity of a crowd.

"Stop! Police!" Barton yelled.

The killer raced up an escalator.

The overweight Barton could not keep pace.

"Stop!"

She ran up to the fifth floor and down a hallway to a railing overlooking the atrium.

By the time Barton made it to the fifth floor and down the hallway, the killer was standing atop a railing. She readied herself to leap to the safety of the fourth floor as each floor was overlapped slightly by the floor above it. Thus, the floor directly below could be reached by a precise leap. It was exactly what Jeffrey Ho had done as he leapt from the floor above to land between the killer and the lieutenant to save Barton's life.

"Stop! Police!" Barton yelled again.

Just as the killer pushed off the fifth-floor railing her foot slipped.

She missed her mark on the fourth floor and plunged to the ground.

Barton rushed to the railing and looked at the body below.

There was no movement and even from that height several floors above Barton could see blood ebbing from the prone, lifeless body.

As Barton removed his hand from the railing, a small amount of the slippery, red, substance was on his hand from the spot on the railing where the killer had stood.

When Barton got downstairs, he checked for a pulse. She was dead.

Barton returned to his friend and knelt in silence on one knee over Jeffrey Ho, and said, "Jeffrey, it's Barton."

Suddenly, Jeffrey opened his eyes. "I thought I should keep my eyes closed and remain absolutely still just in case anyone approached that wasn't you."

Barton grinned, "A good idea, my friend," as Barton helped him to his feet and assisted him in removing the flak jacket. "Are you okay?"

Jeffrey nodded, "I think so...that is, if this isn't my blood."

"Let's see," he said, as he began to remove the fake neck that Hollywood makeup artist Pete had designed especially for Jeffrey.

A metal protector covered the neck while around it was a fleshy-like padding filled with a liquid...fake blood but realistic. It was something Pete had designed for his Hollywood slasher movies. When the padding was cut, it spurted the blood while a thin layer of metal protected the actor, though of course, in the movies the knife used was not a real one. With the makeup Pete applied over the device, the killer couldn't have known Jeffrey was wearing protection...just like in the movies.

Once the protective gear was fully removed, Barton examined Jeffrey's neck, and said, "You're okay...not even a nick," as he helped Jeffrey to his feet.

"And the killer? Did you get her?"

"She got herself. It's over."

The End

Epilogue

That evening Lieutenant Barton and Jeffrey Ho had a couple of drinks together. Though Jeffrey continued his choice of non-alcoholic refreshment, Barton opted otherwise since the case was now closed.

"What's this again?" Barton asked.

"That's a Singapore Sling," Jeffrey answered. "It was invented right here."

"And what's the name of this place again?"

"This is the Raffles Hotel."

"Ah," Barton replied, as he took another sip.

"Are you still a bit shaken?" Barton asked.

"More than a bit," Jeffrey nodded awkwardly.

"That was very courageous that you did. You've got a lot of guts, my friend," as Barton observed Jeffrey's hand trembling slightly as he lifted his drink to his lips.

"All my previous work with the Singapore Police was on the informational side, whatever intelligence my psychic ability could provide. I think this'll be the last time I do anything like this again."

Barton nodded, "Probably wise."

"As you're aware, I knew Catherine Lim but I had never met her sister. How did you figure it went down?" Jeffrey inquired.

"Well, during my meeting with Catherine Lim, I didn't conduct an interview or interrogation as such. I kept it on a friendly, casual basis. I said I merely wanted to thank her in person for requesting my assistance on the case because I always enjoy getting out of the office in Chicago."

When a skeptical look crossed Jeffrey's face, Barton added, "That was the ruse for putting her off guard and getting her to be open with me. Anyway, I was showing Catherine a picture of my family and she in turn showed me a pic of her family... herself, her parents and her sister."

"Yes, when I stepped away to make some calls, I noticed you were showing her your phone, and I was meaning to ask you about that."

"It turned out that it was Catherine's sister who said, 'Too bad you can't get someone like the famous Cy Barton, the Chicago detective, who travels to various destinations to assist in murder investigations,' or words to that effect. It was her sister, Jennifer, who planted the idea in Catherine's mind."

"When did she say that?"

"Shortly after the second murder...and later after the fourth murder...Catherine suggested it to the Prime Minister. I knew then it was one of them...Catherine or Jennifer Lim, and I'd suspected almost from the get-go the killer was a woman."

"What made you think so?"

"How easily the police were approached."

"Oh," Jeffrey nodded in acknowledgment though he wasn't completely following the lieutenant's train of thought.

"All the victims were male and all of them were single."

"You think a single male would be more easily approachable than one who is married?"

"If a woman was approaching them, absolutely!" Barton replied without hesitation. "And, if I was right, she would be about 5' 7" or 5' 8" tall.

"Tall for a woman in this part of the world, but that narrowed the number of suspects considerably," Jeffrey smiled.

"Yes, and a woman could approach them without suspicion...would take them off guard...and who at least once had asked one of the victims for a light as she did with me at the mall."

"The cigarette lighter beside one of the victims," Jeffrey offered.

"Yes," Barton confirmed. "She used her beauty as a tool...a tool to get in close for the kill. Perhaps four of the victims informed her as she neared them that smoking was not allowed; but she continued to approach and closed in on her prey. One victim pulled out his lighter. Perhaps he told her to take it and step outside to light her cigarette or maybe his male hormones got the better of him and he offered to light her cigarette on the spot.

Jeffrey emitted a long sigh as he shook his head.

"Though Catherine loved her sister, they weren't close. In age, they were six years apart and Catherine understood the pressure Jennifer was under to 'measure up' to her older sister, and Catherine always watched out for her, helped her. As the years passed, Catherine thought things were getting better between them," Barton explained, as he took a slug of his drink and continued.

"From what we've pieced together Catherine was the gifted one in the family...better student...brighter...more popular. We learned that Jennifer was always jealous of Catherine. When they were younger, Catherine was always a little bit better than Jennifer in everything, that is in everything except soccer. It was in soccer that Jennifer exceled. A former star athlete she was so good she was going to be on the Singapore soccer team in the Olympics until an injury had ended any hope of competing. She had a promising future in the sport and could have turned professional but it was a career-ending knee injury. With that injury Jennifer descended into depression and wallowed in self-pity which served to feed the jealousy she felt toward her older sister more."

Jeffrey shook his head, "If not for that injury...,"

Barton nodded as Jeffrey didn't need to explain what he was thinking.

"Eventually, Catherine got Jennifer a job in the civil service, but Jennifer didn't do very well. Though she got promoted after two years, it turned out to be her only promotion in eight years."

"That certainly must have damaged her ego," Jeffrey offered.

"Yes," Barton agreed, "and it didn't help that she owed her job to her older sister, but it was during her time as a civil servant that Jennifer became interested in psychic phenomena. When we spoke to her parents, they confirmed they thought Jennifer may have had a psychic gift as a child but it wasn't pursued. Well, she pursued it as an adult.

Jennifer studied and practiced to develop her gift to its fullest potential. She wanted to use her gift to get back at her sister...to embarrass her in some way...and she was very diabolical about it."

"Yeah, diabolical is right," echoed Jeffrey.

"As she watched her sister's career blossom, Jennifer's jealousy increased. Eventually, her jealousy turned to hatred, and she was most assuredly quite insane. The murdering of Singapore policemen was for no other reason than to embarrass her sister.

Jeffrey shook his head and his body seemed to shake as well at the very thought of that.

"Jennifer devised her plan and when she was ready, she began killing. When the murders went unsolved, it was Jennifer who subtlety planted the idea in her sister's mind that Catherine should suggest to the Prime Minister the 'famous' Lieutenant Barton be called into the case for assistance."

"Why? Why were you part of her plan?"

Barton shrugged, "I don't really know but my gut tells me to simply feed her ego when a renowned homicide detective is killed trying to help the Singapore authorities catch the killer. My guess is it didn't really matter if I was sent on this assignment or not...but it would have been a bonus for her."

Jeffrey shook his head again and took a big gulp from his drink, and asked, "But why kill Singapore policemen?"

"The greater embarrassment to the Singapore government, the greater the embarrassment to Catherine."

Jeffrey let out an exasperating gasp, "That truly is insane. It's all so sick," said Jeffrey.

"Yeah, the demented mind of a serial killer and you know, Jeffrey, the sad thing is that Jennifer Lim may have succeeded in destroying her sister."

"What do you mean?"

"Now that everyone knows who committed the murders, I don't think Catherine Lim will rise any higher in the Singapore government, not with this in her family background. She's already taken a leave of absence...per the request of the Prime Minister."

"That's really too bad, lieutenant."

Barton nodded in agreement, "Yeah," he said, and upon reflection added, "and Jennifer Lim destroyed more than her sister and the five lives she took. She also destroyed the families of those five police officers, the parents, brothers, sisters...they'll all miss them. Those families will never be the same again."

"And, I'm afraid," Jeffrey interjected, "Singapore may never be quite the same again either. Jennifer Lim was our first serial killer."

"Yeah," Barton nodded, "sometimes it's a real sick world, but thanks to you, Jeffrey, at least we stopped the killings."

The next morning Barton stood in line to board the flight home...via Japan and San Francisco of course. As he waited in the slow-moving line, he kept thinking about that long flight home. His shoulders slumped and a look of disgust crossed his face as he thought about how grueling that flight would be...just a few days after he arrived.

"The hell with this!" he said to himself, as he turned away.

He would phone Sharon later in the day. She would understand, but for now he pulled out his cell and called someone else.

He heard a voice answer on the other end of the line, "Jeffrey here."

"Hey, Jeffrey," Barton smiled.

"Lieutenant?"

"We're not working a case any longer so please, call me, Cy. What was that you said about seeing some of the sights of Singapore?"

About the Author

Bob has also authored full-length novels *Pictures on the Wall*, his initial novel on political courage, *Whispers in the Night* about revenge on a criminal empire and *The Game Begins* about a fictional serial killer.

Raised in Downers Grove, Illinois, Bob is a graduate of the University of Oklahoma and lives in Glenview, Illinois with his long-time companion, Mary Ellen.